WELCOME TO

RAVENS PASS

BITES

by Steve Brezenoff
illustrated by Amerigo Pinelli

Ravens Pass is published by Stone Arch Books
a Capstone imprint
1710 Roe Crest Drive
North Mankato, Minnesota 56003
www.capstonepub.com

Cataloging-in-Publication Data is available at the Library of
Congress website.
ISBN: 978-1-4342-4617-2 (library binding)
ISBN: 978-1-4342-6217-2 (paperback)

Summary: Do vampires really exist in Ravens Pass? Collin, the
new kid in school, doesn't think so — until a new friend gives
him a tour of town . . .

Graphic Designer: Hilary Wacholz
Art Director: Kay Fraser

Photo credits:
iStockphoto: chromatika (sign, back cover); spxChrome (torn
paper, pp. 7, 13, 17, 35, 43, 51, 61, 69, 65)
Shutterstock: Milos Luzanin (newspaper, pp. 92, 93, 94, 95,
96); Robyn Mackenzie (torn ad, pp. 1, 2, 96); Tischenko Irina
(sign, pp. 1, 2).

Printed in China by Nordica
0413/CA21300450
032013   007226NORDF13

Between where you live and where you've been, there is a town. It lies along the highway, and off the beaten path. It's in the middle of a forest, and in the middle of a desert. It's on the shore of a lake, and along a raging river. It's surrounded by mountains, and on the edge of a deadly cliff. If you're looking for it, you'll never find it, but if you're lost, it'll appear on your path.

The town is **RAVENS PASS,** and you might never leave.

TABLE OF CONTENTS

Chapter 1
THE NEW KID

Collin was the new kid at school — again. Being the new kid was never fun. Collin's family had moved around plenty, always for the same reasons. He was only twelve, and he'd lived in seven different cities and attended seven different schools. But Ravens Pass seemed stranger than the others.

Like usual, at this school every one of his teachers made him stand at the front of the room and introduce himself. Math, his last class of the day, was no different than the others.

"Welcome, Collin," his math teacher said after Collin told her his name and handed her the forms he'd been carrying from class to class.

Collin headed for a desk at the back, hoping that would be the end of the matter. The teacher cleared her throat. "Would you please come up to the front, Collin?" she asked.

Collin sighed and walked back to her desk. Standing in front of all his classmates, he said, "My name's Collin Bertram. I just moved here from River City. I enjoy lion taming and hang gliding."

Collin liked to see if the kids were paying attention while he introduced himself. They almost never were. But Ravens Pass was different from any other new town he'd moved to. In most classes, in most cities, the kids didn't listen to him.

In fact, most of the time, the other students talked to each other, threw balled-up paper around the room, or played with their phones. Sometimes they'd just giggle and whisper to each other.

But in Ravens Pass, they all stared at Collin after he spoke. They didn't smile. They didn't laugh. They didn't whisper. They just stared.

Collin hurried back to a desk at the back of the room. No one spoke until the teacher started the lesson. In fact, everyone seemed tired. Or scared.

"Psst," said the boy next to Collin.

Collin looked up from his desk. "Me?" he said.

The boy kept his eyes on his notebook as he nodded. "You should tell your family to move back to River City," he said.

"Why?" Collin asked. "Is this place all that bad?"

The boy looked around nervously. "I guess you haven't heard yet," he said.

Collin leaned closer to the other boy. "Heard what?" he asked. He glanced at the teacher. She was scribbling a formula on the whiteboard with her back to the class.

The other boy glanced left and right nervously. Then he locked eyes with Collin. "Vampire attacks," he whispered.

Chapter 2
VAMPIRES?

"Vampire attacks?" Collin repeated, a little too loudly.

The teacher dropped her marker. The whole class turned in their seats to stare at Collin.

The other boy snickered.

"Sorry," Collin said, his face flushing red.

No whispers. No giggles. The teacher just picked up her marker and went back to writing on the board.

"Thanks a lot," Collin whispered to the boy.

"I didn't mean to embarrass you," the other boy said. "And I wasn't joking."

"Yeah, right," Collin said. He started copying down the work from the board.

"I really wasn't," the other boy said. "Notice anything strange about the other kids in class?"

Collin scanned the room. The other kids were scribbling notes and listening to the teacher.

"Yeah," Collin said. "Everyone is paying attention. Except us."

The boy chuckled quietly. "That's not what I meant," he said. "Doesn't it seem . . . cold in here?"

Collin squinted at him. "No," he said. "It's pretty warm, actually. The heat is on."

"I agree," the other boy said. "So why are three kids in here wearing scarves?"

Collin looked around. "You're right," he said.

"And where do vampires bite?" the boy asked.

Collin rolled his eyes. "You think those people have vampire bites?" he asked.

"Of course not," the boy said with a smirk. "There's no such thing as vampires."

Collin slumped in his chair. "Then why are they wearing scarves?" he asked.

"That's the mystery," the boy said. "And I intend to solve it. Do you want to help?"

Collin frowned.

"That is, unless you're scared," the boy said.

"I'm not scared," Collin said. "Sure, I'll help."

"Good," the boy said. "I'm Simon Morris, by the way."

Chapter 3
ON THE CASE

Collin and Simon walked through the main hall of Ravens Pass Middle School. The late afternoon sun shined in through the front windows.

"So, where do we start?" Collin asked.

Before they reached the door, Simon stopped. "We should talk to one of the possible victims," he said. "Sammy is in the chess club. This way."

He grabbed Collin's arm and pulled him into the science wing. "The chess club meets down here," Simon said.

"Okay," Collin said. "I hope this won't take too long. My mom thinks I'm going straight home."

"You worry too much," Simon said.

Simon led Collin down the quiet science hallway. All the classrooms were empty, and most of them were dark.

At the last classroom, Simon knocked on the closed door. Then he swung it open.

Inside, six boys sat in pairs at tables. Chess sets were between them. A teacher in a wrinkly old suit sat at the big desk in the back. His eyes were closed, and he was snoring quietly.

"Sammy," Simon hissed into the quiet room.

A shaggy-haired boy with glasses looked up from his game.

"Can we talk to you?" Simon said.

Sammy got up and walked over to the door. He wore a turtleneck sweater, even though the chess room was warm.

"What?" Sammy said when he reached them.

"This is Collin," Simon said. "Show him your neck."

"Seriously?" Sammy said. "I'm in the middle of an important match."

"Show him," Simon said.

"We're out to solve the mystery," Collin added.

Sammy frowned. "What mystery?" he said. "I got attacked by a vampire. I'm lucky to be alive. It's not a mystery." He pulled down one side of the neck of his sweater.

On Sammy's throat were two small bite marks.

"Happy?" Sammy asked, letting his turtleneck snap back into place. "Now can I finish my game?"

Simon nodded. He and Collin headed back down the long science hallway.

"Any theories?" Simon asked.

"Yep," Collin said. "He's a vampire. That's my theory."

Simon rolled his eyes. "Not you, too!" hc said. "I take it some other kids have already told you all the myths about Ravens Pass."

Collin nodded. "Yep, during my first class," Collin said. "One boy told me he knows a family of werewolves who lives down by the lake."

Simon laughed.

"And a kid in my English class said a demon lives in the retirement home," Collin said.

Simon shook his head. "I'm surprised no one mentioned the haunted movie theater," he said. "Listen, you're coming with me to visit my great-grandfather."

"Why?" Collin said.

"He's been living here for almost a hundred years," Simon said. "And he'll tell you it's just a normal town — just a city with lots of silly stories."

Collin glanced out the big front doors. The sun was beginning to set. "Right now?" he asked.

"Sure," Simon said. "It's not a long walk to Pine Estate."

"The retirement home?" Collin said. "That's where your great-grandpa lives?"

"Sure," Simon said. "Oh, come on. Don't tell me you believe the demon story."

Collin didn't say anything, but he was thinking about it.

"There are no old demon grandpas at the home," Simon said. "I promise."

Collin took a deep breath. He didn't want a bunch of stories to ruin his life in Ravens Pass. But something was wrong here, he knew that much.

"Okay, you're right," Collin said. "Let me just call my mom so she knows I'll be late."

Chapter 4

SIMON THE FIRST

The sun was just an orange smudge on the horizon by the time the boys left the school.

"It sure does get dark early here," Collin said.

"Only because it's November," Simon said. "The days this summer were so long, we thought they'd never end."

Collin shivered as a cool breeze swept across the back of his neck. The moon was up now — a narrow crescent.

"There it is," Simon said, pointing at the big old brick building on the hill at the end of Main Street.

A wooden sign out front had a spotlight shining on it. The sign read, "Pine Estate Assisted Living."

The boys walked up the long driveway. Collin pulled his jacket tighter around his neck. He shivered when the porch steps creaked. Dry leaves rustled on the sidewalk behind Collin, making him feel like someone was constantly following them.

Collin pushed open the big glass door. Inside, warm yellow light filled the lobby.

A man in white sat behind the counter next to the elevator. "Hello, Simon," he said. "Here to see Simon the First?"

"I sure am, Keith," Simon said. He walked up to the counter and signed his name in the guest book. "I thought he'd like to meet Collin, Ravens Pass's newest resident."

"Hi," Collin said. He signed his name, too.

"Welcome to town," Keith said. Then he looked at Simon. "Has the new boy met any monsters yet?"

Simon and Keith stared at Collin a moment. Then Keith and Simon both burst into laughter.

"Say hi for me," Keith said as the elevator opened.

"Will do," Simon said. Collin followed him into the elevator, and up they went.

"Great-Grandpa is on the third floor," Simon said.

"How many Simons are there?" Collin asked.

"I'm the fourth," said Simon. "All the first-born boys in our family are named Simon, ever since Great-Grandpa."

"Weird," Collin said.

"Yeah, it's tough to live up to," Simon said. "Simon the First is kind of a legend in the family."

The elevator dinged as the doors opened. The boys walked into a brightly lit hallway. The floor was green tile, and the walls were brick. As they walked, Collin noticed the light flickered very fast. The bulbs — the long fluorescent kind — hummed on the ceiling.

The doors they passed looked mostly similar, aside from a few personal touches some residents or their families must have added — like photos of some kids, or Halloween decorations.

Simon stopped in front of the plainest door on the floor. He knocked. "It's me, Great-Grandpa," he called through the closed door.

"Come in," a muffled voice called back. Simon opened the door and the boys went in.

Simon's great-grandfather sat in a big, antique chair in the corner, near a window. The curtains were wide open and the blinds were pulled all the way up. Collin could see the crescent moon and the gray clouds hanging in the window.

"Great-Grandpa," Simon said, "this is Collin. He and his family just moved to Ravens Pass."

The old man stood up from the big chair. "Nice to meet you, Collin," he said.

"I've been trying to convince Collin that the stories about Ravens Pass aren't true," Simon said. "But he's still scared of ghosts and ghouls and goblins."

"I am not," Collin said quickly.

The old man smiled. "What stories have they told you?" he asked.

Collin went down the list again, like he had for Simon. Great-Grandpa nodded after each one.

"So, Great-Grandpa," Simon said. "Tell him how many monsters you've met in Ravens Pass."

"Well, Collin," the old man said. "I had my ninety-ninth birthday recently, and I've spent every one of those years here in Ravens Pass. I have never seen a monster, and I've never met a ghost, and I've never heard a werewolf howling at the moon."

"What did I tell you?" Simon said. "Now, are you ready to actually solve this mystery?"

Collin shrugged. "I guess," he said. He glanced at the clock on the table next to Great-Grandpa's chair. "It's getting late, though. I should probably get home."

"It was nice to meet you, Collin," Great-Grandpa said. He led the boys toward the door. "If any monsters come after you, make sure to give me a call!"

The old man and Simon laughed.

Collin felt his face go red.

Chapter 5

BLOOD

After they left the building, Collin turned toward his neighborhood.

"Where are you going?" Simon asked. "I thought we were going to solve the mystery."

"I told you," Collin said, staring at his feet. "I need to get home. Tomorrow is Saturday. We can spend the whole day solving the mystery."

Simon smirked and shook his head. "Can't," he said. "I have to do all my chores on Saturday. We'd have to meet up very early — like, five in the morning."

Collin couldn't imagine having to spend all day Saturday working around the house. *Simon's parents must be very strict*, he thought. "That's pretty early," Collin said. "The sun won't even be up by then."

Simon put his hands in his pockets. "Nope," he said. "But that's how it is." He looked at Collin and smiled. "Unless you want to check out the crime scene right now? It'll only take a few minutes."

Collin sighed. "Fine," he said. "Just for a few minutes. Then I really have to get home."

"Okay!" Simon said. "This way."

Together, they ran down Second Street toward the playground at the Ravens Pass elementary school.

"Here we are," Simon said. He stopped at the swing set. "This is where the very first supposed vampire attack happened."

Collin looked around. "So what do we do now?" he asked.

"We look for clues," Simon said.

Collin nodded. He looked around again. "Like what?" he asked.

Simon sighed and rolled his eyes. He scanned the ground quickly, then jogged past Collin. "Like this," he said, pointing at the grass near his feet.

Collin hurried over. "What is it?" Collin asked.

The boys squatted down. "This," Simon said, pointing to a little spot on the grass, "and this," he added, pointing to another.

Collin squinted at the ground. "What are they?" he asked.

"Blood droplets," Simon said. "Obviously."

"It doesn't look like blood to me," Collin said.

"Trust me," Simon said. "So this is where the kid was when the attacker got him."

"We knew that already," Collin said.

Simon ignored him and started prowling along the row of hedges nearby. He was bent at the waist, looking at the ground.

"Looking for more blood?" Collin called to him.

Simon shook his head. "If I attacked someone where you're standing," he said, "I'd toss the weapon into these bushes."

"What weapon?" Collin asked. "Vampires use their teeth."

"For the last time," Simon said, stopping, "there's no such thing as vampires!"

Simon knelt down next to the bushes. He picked something up. "Come look at this," he said.

Collin strolled over. Simon was holding a small pencil. The point was broken off.

"So?" Collin said. "It's a little pencil. This is a school playground. Students use pencils."

"I think this pencil was used to stab someone in the neck," Simon said. "Twice, so it would look like tooth marks."

"Yeah, right," Collin said. "What kid would mistake a weirdo with a pencil for a vampire?"

Simon tapped the pencil on his palm, thinking. "We should interview the first victim," he said. "She's a neighbor of mine."

"Later," Collin said. "I have to go home now."

Simon nodded. "Okay, you're right," he said. "We'll talk tomorrow after I'm finished with my chores."

Chapter 6
TOOTHPICKS?

Collin looked at the display of his cell phone. He definitely didn't recognize the number. "Who is this?" he asked.

"It's me," the voice said impatiently. "Simon. There's been another vampire attack."

Collin yawned. "What time is it?" he asked.

"It's almost five in the morning," Simon said. "We have to hurry so I can get home for chores."

Collin yawned again. "Fine," he said. "Where should we meet?"

"Behind the middle school, near the basketball courts," Simon said. "Hurry!" Then he hung up.

* * *

It was very chilly and dark. Collin shivered as he walked through Ravens Pass. He wished he'd put on something warmer than a long-sleeve shirt.

Collin got to the school just after five. Simon was already there, kneeling by the edge of the basketball court.

"Finally," Simon called out when he spotted Collin. "Look what I found."

"What?" Collin said, squatting next to Simon.

"Look how messed up the grass is," said Simon. "Check out the smudges and footprints in the dirt."

"So?" Collin said. He yawned. "It's a playground. Footprints will be everywhere."

"Don't you see?" Simon asked. "This is where the attack must have happened."

"It's the edge of the court," Collin said. "This could just be where a ball went out of bounds."

"Maybe," Simon admitted.

"Did you find a pencil?" Collin asked.

Simon shook his head. "Not yet," he said. He hurried over to a row of bushes. He reached deep into the bushes and pulled out a little paper box. "Aha!" he said.

Collin jogged over to Simon. "Toothpicks?" Collin asked. "So what?"

Simon opened the box and poked at the little sticks of wood. "None of them have blood on them," he said. "But these are probably the ones the culprit didn't use."

Collin shook his head. "Maybe," he said. "But they're pretty small. The holes they'd make in a neck wouldn't look right."

"You didn't see the first victim's neck marks," Simon said. "They were very small."

"You saw the first victim's bite marks?" Collin asked.

"That's how I knew about all of this," Simon said. "The girl who got bit is my neighbor."

Collin shivered as a gust of cold wind blew by him. "Is she okay?" he asked.

"She told me she screamed when it happened," Simon said. "And then she passed out. The attacker must have run off when she screamed."

"She didn't see who it was?" Collin asked, turning to look at the horizon.

"Nope," Simon said.

Collin glanced upward. "The sun is rising," he said. "If I'm not home when my parents get up, I'll get in trouble."

Simon frowned. "Oh, yeah," he said, standing up. "I have to get home, too. And quick."

"Chores, huh?" Collin said.

Simon pulled out his cell phone to check the time. "Huh?" he said. "Oh, yeah, chores. I'll see you later."

Simon glanced at the horizon, and then dashed across the field toward his house.

Collin hurried back toward his house. He was back in his bed by sunrise.

Chapter 7

THE GIRL NEXT DOOR

When Collin woke up, it was past noon. He could hear his little sister running around downstairs, complaining that nothing was on TV.

Collin sat up in bed and held his stomach. He hadn't eaten in a while.

"Hungry," he mumbled. He grabbed the phone and redialed the last incoming call: Simon's phone.

It rang and rang, and finally Simon's voice mail picked up. "It's Collin," he said. "Um, call me when you're done with chores."

Collin pulled back the blinds in his room. It was a gray, overcast day. There was no sunshine at all.

Downstairs, he could hear his little sister storming around the house, screaming her lungs out. That could go on all day. He'd have to get out or go crazy.

Collin decided to find that girl — the one who got attacked in the night. She was Simon's next-door neighbor. It shouldn't be hard to find her.

* * *

It was raining hard by the time Collin reached the other side of Ravens Pass. He stuck to the sidewalks, under shop awnings and big maples still holding on to their orange and yellow leaves. Even so, the rain found him. He was wet by the time he reached Simon's neighborhood.

Collin had found Simon's address online, but it wasn't easy. There was no listing under Simon Morris, or Simon Morris the Third, which Collin figured was his dad's name. He finally found an old newspaper article about the town's history. It showed Simon the First's address back when he was a kid. Collin guessed the Morrises still lived there. He was right.

He stood on the sidewalk in front of the house. The house was dark. All the shades were pulled. There was no car in the driveway.

"I thought he had chores to do all day," Collin muttered to himself. "So why does it look like the whole family is gone?"

He thought about knocking on the door, or even going around back to try to peek in the windows.

But Collin figured it was kind of weird to go peeking through windows. Instead, he picked one of the next-door neighbors — there were two, one on each side — and knocked on their door.

A voice came from behind the closed door. "Who is it?" it said in a thick whisper. "Just go away!"

"I'm sorry," Collin said. "I'm looking for —" He didn't know the girl's name.

"Go away!" the voice said again, this time much louder. "Go away or I'll call the police!"

"I'm sorry!" Collin repeated. Then he ran from the door, past the Morrises' house, to the other next-door neighbor.

He knocked. This time, there was no frightened angry voice. Instead there were light and quick footsteps, and the door swung open.

"Hello," said the girl at the door. She was a little older than Collin, maybe a student at the high school. She wore a red ribbon around her neck.

"Who are you?" she asked.

"I'm Collin," he said. "I'm a friend of Simon Morris, your next-door neighbor."

She pulled back her head and squinted at him. "That kid has friends?" she asked.

"He goes to school with me," Collin said.

The girl shrugged. "If you say so," she said. "So what do you want?"

Collin pointed at her neck. "That's an interesting ribbon," he said.

Her face lit up. She ran a finger along the shimmery red material. "Don't you love it?" she said. "And here's the best part."

The girl pulled down the ribbon just a little to reveal two small red scabs. They were very small. They looked like they really could have been made by those toothpicks.

The girl leaned in close and whispered, "It's a vampire bite."

Colin could smell her toothpaste. "You seem happy about it," he said.

She sighed and put a hand on her heart. "I am," she said wistfully. "It's the most romantic thing I've heard of, you know?"

"What?" Collin said. "Vampires are killers!"

"Do I look dead to you?" she said.

She does look a little pale, Collin thought. Before he could answer, though, she went on, "I wish I could have seen him."

"The vampire?" Collin asked. "You mean you didn't?"

She shook her head once, still smiling. "Nope," she said. "It was too dark, and he snuck up on me. When I screamed and fainted, he must have run away."

"So you don't know who it was?" Collin asked.

The girl's smile faded. "No," she said. Then she sighed. "Why did I have to scream? I must have scared him off."

Without saying good-bye, the girl closed the door in Collin's face.

"Teenage girls are weird," Collin muttered as he turned from the door.

Chapter 8

FAMILY

The rain was much lighter when Collin left Simon's neighborhood. He decided to head home.

The sun was already starting to set by the time Collin reached the corner. He glanced back over his shoulder toward the Morris house.

To his surprise, the front door of the house was open.

"Hey, Collin," Simon shouted from the open doorway. "What are you doing here?"

Collin jogged over. "Where have you been all day?" he asked.

"I told you," Simon said. He looked over Collin's shoulder at the clearing skies to the west. The sun was already below the horizon. "I was doing my chores."

"But your house was dark," Collin said. "It looked like no one was home."

"We were home," Simon insisted. "All day Saturday, every week, sunrise to sundown, we're in here doing dumb chores. So what are you doing here?"

"I decided to interview your neighbor," Collin said. "I mean, about her attack."

"Waste of time," Simon said. "She doesn't remember anything helpful."

"You talked to her already?" Collin asked.

"I heard all about it after it happened," Simon said. "I told you."

"Oh," Collin said.

"Did she tell you herself?" Collin asked.

"Nah," Simon said after a moment. "She told my sister. She was pretty upset."

Just then, a tall girl who looked a lot like Simon came up behind him. "You talking about me, little bro?" she said. She put her arm around his neck in a joking headlock.

"Get off me, Holly," Simon said. She didn't let go, though. "This is Collin," Simon went on. "He's new here. I was just telling him how your friend next door was really upset."

Holly squinted at Simon.

"About being attacked," Simon added.

"Oh yeah," Holly said, looking at Collin. "She was really upset. Crying and everything. She's lucky to be alive."

Collin glanced at Simon, then Holly, then at Simon again.

"Look, I'd better get home," Collin said. "If I'm not back for dinner . . ."

"You'll be in big trouble, young man!" Holly said. She and Simon laughed.

"Yeah," Collin said, backing away. "So, see you."

"Don't you want to do some more investigating?" Simon asked. "I'm all done with my chores now."

"No," Collin said. "I really have to get home. But I think you were right about the toothpicks."

"See?" Simon said. "Stick with me. We'll crack this case."

Collin watched as Holly and Simon turned and walked off. As the door slowly swung closed, he could see the big stairway in the middle of the house, and a little of the downstairs hallway. Everything looked dusty and dirty, and there were spider webs on the banister.

I guess their chores don't include cleaning the house, Collin thought.

Chapter 9
PINE ESTATE

By Sunday evening, Collin still hadn't heard from Simon. He tried calling Simon's phone once after lunch, but there was no answer. He figured the Morrises did chores on Sunday too.

"Or maybe they go to church," Collin muttered to himself. "And then lunch." For some reason, he didn't think that was true.

He tapped his pencil on his notebook, struggling with his homework assignment. It was due in the morning, and the math was taking forever.

Collin watched the tip of the pencil bounce on the blank page of his notebook. *Could a pencil like this one really be responsible for those bite marks?* he thought. *Something doesn't seem right.*

The phone rang. Collin grabbed it quickly. It was Simon.

"Hello?" Collin said.

"There's been another . . . attack," Simon said. He was out of breath, and he gasped for air between the words.

"Where are you?" Collin asked. "Are you running?"

"Yes," Simon said. "Hurry. Meet me at Pine Estate." Then he hung up.

Collin checked the time on the clock on his bedroom wall. It was late, and it was Sunday.

Collin's parents would never let him go out now. Not without a very good reason.

Collin ran downstairs to where his parents and sister were sitting in the den. He stood in front of the TV to get their attention.

"I'm having a lot of trouble with my math homework," Collin said. His four-year-old sister, Lolli, was watching a cartoon about a talking ice cream cone. It was her favorite.

"Can we help?" his dad asked.

Collin had expected that question. He held out his math textbook to a page filled with mathematical formulae and complicated questions. His dad looked at it for a few moments, then frowned.

"This is over my head," Dad said.

"I called someone from class," Collin said. "His name is Simon Morris. I can walk over there. It's okay with his parents if it's okay with you two."

His mom sighed. Dad laughed. "It's okay with me," Dad said.

"Fine," Mom said. "But I want you home by 9:30 at the very latest. Are we clear?"

"Clear!" Collin said and ran out the door. Sprinting up Main Street toward the old building on the hill, he saw that there were no stars in the sky and no moon. The night was pitch black. Only thick dark clouds and pale spotlight pointed at that wooden sign: Pine Estate.

Chapter 10

THE MORRISES

Three Morrises stood in the lobby: Simon the First, Simon the Fourth, and Holly. In a chair nearby was Keith, the guard.

Collin ran up to them, out of breath. "Is Keith the attacker?" he asked.

The Morrises laughed.

"Of course not," Great-Grandpa said. He stood with his hands behind him and his chin up, so he could look down his nose at Collin. "This is the newest victim of the joker."

"Huh," Collin said. "A big guy like you? I would've thought you could put up a fight. You saw who did it at least, right?"

Keith's face went a little red. "I'm sorry to say," he said, "but I must have nodded off."

Great-Grandpa chuckled. "Asleep on the job, Keith?" he said.

Keith shook his head sadly. "You know, we've got a new puppy at home," he said. "I was up four times to take him outside last night."

"But someone poked you in the neck," Collin said. "Didn't that wake you up?"

Keith shrugged. "All I know is that when I woke up," the guard said, "Simon the First here was standing over me. He said he heard me shouting as he was coming down the elevator."

"Coming down the elevator?" Collin said, looking at Great-Grandpa. "Where were you going?"

Great-Grandpa thought for a moment. "I was coming downstairs to meet my grandchildren, as you can see," he said, gesturing toward the younger Simon and Holly. "I have supper with Simon and Holly every Sunday night."

Keith, with his hand on his neck, nodded. "It's true," he said. "He does."

"Wow, this guy really got you bad, huh?" Collin said, stepping closer to the guard. "Can I, um, see the marks?"

Gingerly, Keith pulled his hand away from his throat. "Is it bad?" he said. "These three won't let me check the mirror."

Collin almost gasped. He covered his mouth with his hand. "This is the worst one I've seen," he said quietly. He glanced at Simon.

Simon nodded. "I know," he said. "This was no pencil or toothpick."

"I think this is getting pretty serious," Collin said, standing up straight and facing each of the Morrises in turn. "We need to call the police or something."

Simon and Holly both started to speak, but Great-Grandpa silenced them with a wave of his hand. "I don't think that's necessary," he said, smiling at Collin.

For the first time, Collin noticed the one sign of age on Great-Grandpa: his teeth. Most of his teeth looked like they'd been rotting away for years. But his incisors were sharp and pointy.

"It's just some practical joke that got a little out of hand," Great-grandpa went on. "I'm sure we can handle this ourselves." He stared right into Collin's eyes.

"Out of hand?" Collin said, trying to return Great-grandpa's gaze. "It looks like someone attacked Keith with a screwdriver or something, and Keith is a big guy. This attacker is dangerous."

"Look, can I go now?" Keith said. "If it's as bad as the kid says, I should get to the hospital."

He started to get up, but with a firm hand, Holly pushed him back into his chair. "I doubt it's that serious," she said. "I'll get something from the first-aid kid and clean it right up."

Holly headed into the office behind where they were standing.

"I'd better go home," Collin said. "Um, Simon, can I use your cell phone? In my rush out of the house, I forgot mine."

"What for?" Simon said, pulling the phone out of his pocket. "You're not thinking of calling the cops, are you?"

"Oh no," Collin said. He tried to laugh. "Just my mom, so she can come pick me up."

Simon smirked. "Why do you need a ride?" he said. "It's not a long walk. In fact, why don't you come to supper with Great-Grandpa and me and Holly?"

"I really can't," Collin said. He kept his eyes on the cell phone, still in Simon's closed fist. "I have to be home by . . . nine."

Great-Grandpa stepped up to Collin.

Great-Grandpa put a hand on Collin's shoulder and looked down at him with his long, stern face.

"Here's the thing, boy," Great-Grandpa said quietly. He glanced back at Keith, who was squirming in his seat, trying to watch what Holly was doing with the bandage. Collin tried to get a look, too. For a moment, it looked like she was blotting the wound and saving the bandages. But that didn't make sense.

Great-Grandpa shifted a little to block Collin's view. "As I was saying," Great-Grandpa went on, "we've been talking about these attacks quite a lot, we Morrises."

"I bet you have," Collin muttered.

Great-Grandpa sneered, briefly showing his stained teeth.

"And we noticed something unusual," the old man said. "The attacks started the very same day you and your family moved to Ravens Pass. Strange, isn't it?"

"Did they?" Collin said. "What a funny coincidence."

"Indeed," Great-Grandpa said. "It would be a shame, wouldn't it, if the people of Ravens Pass learned that . . . well, that someone like you was living here."

Collin laughed nervously. "Like me?" he said. "Don't you mean, like you?"

"Hmm," Great-Grandpa said, pretending to think about it. "Little tiny bite marks, like your sister might make."

"Or Simon," Collin countered.

"Then what about the so-called pencil marks?" Great-Grandpa went on. "Perfectly matched to your teeth, I should think."

"Or Holly's," Collin said.

"And your father," Great-Grandpa said. "His teeth must be quite large."

"As big as yours, I have no doubt," Collin said. He smiled.

"This town," Great-Grandpa said, leaning close to Collin's face, "isn't big enough for the Morrises and the Bertrams."

"No," Collin said, reaching for the door. "I guess it isn't."

* * *

Collin hurried down Main Street till he reached the old drugstore on the corner of 3rd Street.

The drugstore was closed, but he needed the phone booth out front. He called collect.

"Mom?" he said into the phone. "Can you come pick me up? I'm at Third Street and Main, outside the old drugstore."

He listened while she sighed and agreed.

"And one more thing," Collin said. "We're going to have to move again. This town already has a vampire family."

ABOUT THE AUTHOR

STEVE BREZENOFF lives in Minneapolis, Minnesota, with his wife, Beth, and their son, Sam. Besides writing books, he enjoys playing video games, riding his bicycle, and helping middle-school students to improve their writing skills. Steve's ideas almost always come to him in his dreams, so he does his best writing in his pajamas.

ABOUT THE ILLUSTRATOR

A long time ago, when **AMERIGO PINELLI** was very small, his mother gave him a pencil. From that moment on, drawing became his world. Nowadays, Amerigo works as an illustrator above the narrow streets and churches of Naples, Italy. He loves his job because it feels more like play than work. And each morning, as the sun rises over Mount Vesuvius, Amerigo gets to chase pigeons along the rooftops. Just ask his lovely wife, Giulia, if you don't believe him.

GLOSSARY

ANTIQUE (an-TEEK)—a very old object that is valuable because it is rare or beautiful

CULPRIT (KUHL-prit)—a person who is guilty of doing something wrong or of committing a crime

FLUORESCENT (fluh-RESS-uhnt)—giving out a bright light by using a certain type of energy, like ultraviolet light

FORMULAE (FOR myuh-lee)—rules in science or math that are written with numbers and symbols

HORIZON (huh-RYE-zuhn)—the line where the sky and the earth or sea seem to meet

OVERCAST (OH-vur-kast)—an overcast sky is covered with clouds

THEORY (THEER-ee)—an idea or a statement that explains how or why something happens

WISTFULLY (WIST-fuhl-ee)—sadly wishful or longingly

DISCUSSION QUESTIONS

1. Which character did you think was the vampire before the ending of this book — Simon, Collin, or someone else? Why?

2. In this series, Ravens Pass is a town where crazy things happen. Has anything spooky or creepy ever happened in your town? Talk about scary stories you know.

3. Can you think of any other explanations for the creepy things that happen in this book? Discuss your ideas.

WRITING PROMPTS

1. What happens next? Write another chapter that extends this book.

2. How would you have solved the case of the supposed vampire attacks in Ravens Pass? Write about what you would have done differently to find out what really happened.

3. Write a newspaper article describing the events in this book. What might a reporter have to say about the two vampire families in Ravens Pass?

THE CROW'S

BITE-Y OR BATTY?

Rumors are swirling that a vampire family has taken up residence in Ravens Pass. Strange things are common in this city, but I'd never turn down the opportunity to do vampire-related investigative reporting.

While it's true that the Bertram family is rarely seen outside their home during the day, both parents claim to be working night shifts at their jobs.

Also, the recent rash of neck-related bites centers around the Bertram family residence. Stranger still, none of the victims have been able to identify the attackers. The culprits are either very fast or very sneaky.

When I spoke to Collin Bertram about the matter, he denied that he was a vampire but didn't rule out the

EYE

possibility that one, or several vampires, lived somewhere in Ravens Pass. He also told me that his family was considering moving because of all the accusations the Bertrams have received over the past few weeks.

So I turn to you, my clever readers. Are vampires getting bite-y in Ravens Pass, or are the Bertrams just a little batty? You be the judge.

Vampire or normal teenager?

MORE
DARK TALES

FROM RAVENS PASS